The Snow Queen

The Snow Queen

WITH ORIGINAL ILLUSTRATIONS

Hans Christian Andersen

Illustrations by
Vilhelm Pedersen

Translation by
H.B. Paull

2013

The Snow Queen (*Snedronnigen*) was first published, with Pedersen's
illustrations, in 1845. H.B. Paull's translation first appeared in
Hans Andersen's Fairy Tales, 1867, published by Scribner and Co.

Contents

Story the First,

Which Describes a Looking-Glass and the Broken Fragments

You must attend to the commencement of this story, for when we get to the end we shall know more than we do now about a very wicked hobgoblin; he was one of the very worst, for he was a real demon.

One day, when he was in a merry mood, he made a looking-glass which had the power of making everything good or beautiful that was reflected in it almost shrink to nothing, while everything that was worthless and bad looked increased in size and worse than ever. The most lovely landscapes appeared like boiled spinach, and the people became hideous, and looked as if they stood on their heads and had no bodies. Their countenances were so distorted that no one could recognize them, and even one freckle on the face appeared to spread over the whole of the nose and mouth. The demon said this was very amusing. When a good or pious thought passed through the mind of any one it was misrepresented in the glass; and then how the demon laughed at his cunning invention.

All who went to the demon's school—for he kept a school—talked everywhere of the wonders they had seen, and declared that people could now, for the first

time, see what the world and mankind were really like. They carried the glass about everywhere, till at last there was not a land nor a people who had not been looked at through this distorted mirror. They wanted even to fly with it up to heaven to see the angels, but the higher they flew the more slippery the glass became, and they could scarcely hold it, till at last it slipped from their hands, fell to the earth, and was broken into millions of pieces.

But now the looking-glass caused more unhappiness than ever, for some of the fragments were not so large as a grain of sand, and they flew about the world into every country. When one of these tiny atoms flew into a person's eye, it stuck there unknown to him, and from that moment he saw everything through a distorted medium, or could see only the worst side of what he looked at, for even the smallest fragment retained the same power which had belonged to the whole mirror. Some few persons even got a fragment of the looking-glass in their hearts, and this was very terrible, for their hearts became cold like a lump of ice. A few of the pieces were so large that they could be used as window-panes; it would have been a sad thing to look at our friends through them. Other pieces were made into spectacles; this was dreadful for those who wore them, for they could see nothing either rightly or justly.

At all this the wicked demon laughed till his sides shook—it tickled him so to see the mischief he had done. There were still a number of these little fragments of glass floating about in the air, and now you shall hear what happened with one of them.

Second Story,

A Little Boy and a Little Girl

I N a large town, full of houses and people, there is not room for everybody to have even a little garden, therefore they are obliged to be satisfied with a few flowers in flower-pots. In one of these large towns lived two poor children who had a garden something larger and better than a few flower-pots. They were not brother and sister, but they loved each other almost as much as if they had been.

Their parents lived opposite to each other in two garrets, where the roofs of neighboring houses projected out towards each other and the water-pipe ran between them. In each house was a little window, so that anyone could step across the gutter from one window to the other. The parents of these children had each a large wooden box in which they cultivated kitchen herbs for their own use, and a little rose-bush in each box, which grew splendidly.

Now after a while the parents decided to place these two boxes across the water-pipe, so that they reached from one window to the other and looked like two banks of flowers. Sweet-peas drooped over the boxes, and the rose-bushes shot forth long branches, which were trained round the windows and clustered together almost like a triumphal arch of leaves and flowers. The boxes were very high, and the children knew they must not climb upon them, without permission, but they were often, however, allowed to step out together and sit upon their little stools under the rose-bushes, or play quietly.

In winter all this pleasure came to an end, for the windows were sometimes quite frozen over. But then they would warm copper pennies on the stove, and hold the warm pennies against the frozen pane; there would be very soon a little round hole through which they could peep, and the soft bright eyes of the little boy and girl would beam through the hole at each window as they looked at each other.

Their names were Kay and Gerda. In summer they could be together with one jump from the window, but in winter they had to go up and down the long staircase, and out through the snow before they could meet.

"See there are the white bees swarming," said Kay's old grandmother one day when it was snowing.

"Have they a queen bee?" asked the little boy, for he knew that the real bees had a queen.

"To be sure they have," said the grandmother. "She is flying there where the swarm is thickest. She is the largest of them all, and never remains on the earth, but flies up to the dark clouds. Often at midnight she flies through the streets of the town, and looks in at the windows, then the ice freezes on the panes into wonderful shapes, that look like flowers and castles."

"Yes, I have seen them," said both the children, and they knew it must be true.

"Can the Snow Queen come in here?" asked the little girl.

"Only let her come," said the boy, "I'll set her on the stove and then she'll melt."

Then the grandmother smoothed his hair and told him some more tales.

One evening, when little Kay was at home, half undressed, he climbed on a chair by the window and peeped out through the little hole. A few flakes of snow were falling, and one of them, rather larger than the rest, alighted on the edge of one of the flower boxes. This snow-flake grew larger and larger, till at last it became the figure of a woman, dressed in garments of white gauze, which looked like millions of starry snow-flakes linked together. She was fair and beautiful, but made of ice—shining and glittering ice. Still she was alive and her eyes sparkled like bright stars, but there was neither peace nor rest in their glance. She nodded towards the window and waved her hand. The little boy was frightened and sprang from the chair; at the same moment it seemed as if a large bird flew by the window.

On the following day there was a clear frost, and very soon came the spring. The sun shone; the young green leaves burst forth; the swallows built their nests;

windows were opened, and the children sat once more in the garden on the roof, high above all the other rooms. How beautiful the roses blossomed this summer. The little girl had learnt a hymn in which roses were spoken of, and then she thought of their own roses, and she sang the hymn to the little boy, and he sang too:—

"Roses bloom and cease to be,
But we shall the Christ-child see."

Then the little ones held each other by the hand, and kissed the roses, and looked at the bright sunshine, and spoke to it as if the Christ-child were there. Those were splendid summer days. How beautiful and fresh it was out among the rose-bushes, which seemed as if they would never leave off blooming. One day Kay and Gerda sat looking at a book full of pictures of animals and birds, and then just as the clock in the church tower struck twelve, Kay said, "Oh, something has struck my heart!" and soon after, "There is something in my eye."

The little girl put her arm round his neck, and looked into his eye, but she could see nothing.

"I think it is gone," he said. But it was not gone; it was one of those bits of the looking-glass—that magic mirror, of which we have spoken—the ugly glass which made everything great and good appear small and ugly, while all that was wicked and bad became more visible, and every little fault could be plainly seen. Poor little Kay had also received a small grain in his heart, which very quickly turned to a lump of ice. He felt no more pain, but the glass was there still.

"Why do you cry?" said he at last; "it makes you look ugly. There is nothing the matter with me now. Oh, see!" he cried suddenly, "that rose is worm-eaten, and this one is quite crooked. After all they are ugly roses, just like the box in which they stand," and then he kicked the boxes with his foot, and pulled off the two roses.

"Kay, what are you doing?" cried the little girl; and then, when he saw how frightened she was, he tore off another rose, and jumped through his own window away from little Gerda.

When she afterwards brought out the picture book, he said, "It was only fit for babies in long clothes," and when grandmother told any stories, he would interrupt her with "but;" or, when he could manage it, he would get behind her chair, put on a pair of spectacles, and imitate her very cleverly, to make people laugh. By-and-by he began to mimic the speech and gait of persons in the street. All that was peculiar or disagreeable in a person he would imitate directly, and people said, "That boy will be very clever; he has a remarkable genius." But it was the piece of glass in his eye, and the coldness in his heart, that made him act like this. He would even tease little Gerda, who loved him with all her heart.

His games, too, were quite different; they were not so childish. One winter's day, when it snowed, he brought out a burning-glass, then he held out the tail of his blue coat, and let the snow-flakes fall upon it. "Look in this glass, Gerda," said he; and she saw how every flake of snow was magnified, and looked like a beautiful flower or a glittering star. "Is it not clever?"

said Kay, "and much more interesting than looking at real flowers. There is not a single fault in it, and the snow-flakes are quite perfect till they begin to melt."

Soon after Kay made his appearance in large thick gloves, and with his sledge at his back. He called up stairs to Gerda, "I've got to leave to go into the great square, where the other boys play and ride." And away he went.

In the great square, the boldest among the boys would often tie their sledges to the country people's carts, and go with them a good way. This was capital. But while they were all amusing themselves, and Kay with them, a great sledge came by; it was painted white, and in it sat some one wrapped in a rough white fur, and wearing a white cap. The sledge drove twice round the square, and Kay fastened his own little sledge to it, so that when it went away, he followed with it. It went faster and faster right through the next street, and then the person who drove turned round and nodded pleasantly to Kay, just as if they were acquainted with each other, but whenever Kay wished to loosen his little sledge the driver nodded again, so Kay sat still, and they drove out through the town gate.

Then the snow began to fall so heavily that the little boy could not see a hand's breadth before him, but still they drove on; then he suddenly loosened the cord so that the large sled might go on without him, but it was of no use, his little carriage held fast, and away they went like the wind. Then he called out loudly, but nobody heard him, while the snow beat upon him, and the sledge flew onwards. Every now and then it gave a jump as if it were going over hedges and ditches. The boy was frightened, and tried to say a prayer, but he could remember nothing but the multiplication table.

The snow-flakes became larger and larger, till they appeared like great white chickens. All at once they sprang on one side, the great sledge stopped, and the person who had driven it rose up. The fur and the cap, which were made entirely of snow, fell off, and he saw a lady, tall and white, it was the Snow Queen.

"We have driven well," said she, "but why do you tremble? here, creep into my warm fur." Then she seated him beside her in the sledge, and as she wrapped the fur round him he felt as if he were sinking into a snow drift.

"Are you still cold," she asked, as she kissed him on the forehead. The kiss was colder than ice; it went quite through to his heart, which was already almost a lump of ice; he felt as if he were going to die, but only for a moment; he soon seemed quite well again, and did not notice the cold around him.

"My sledge! don't forget my sledge," was his first thought, and then he looked and saw that it was bound fast to one of the white chickens, which flew behind him with the sledge at its back. The Snow Queen kissed little Kay again, and by this time he had forgotten little Gerda, his grandmother, and all at home.

"Now you must have no more kisses," she said, "or I should kiss you to death."

Kay looked at her, and saw that she was so beautiful, he could not imagine a more lovely and intelligent face; she did not now seem to be made of ice, as when he had seen her through his window, and she had nodded to him. In his eyes she was perfect, and she did not feel at all afraid.

He told her he could do mental arithmetic, as far as fractions, and that he knew the number of square miles and the number of inhabitants in the country. And she always smiled so that he thought he did not know enough yet, and she looked round the vast expanse as she flew higher and higher with him upon a black cloud, while the storm blew and howled as if it were singing old songs.

They flew over woods and lakes, over sea and land; below them roared the wild wind; the wolves howled and the snow crackled; over them flew the black screaming crows, and above all shone the moon, clear and bright,—and so Kay passed through the long winter's night, and by day he slept at the feet of the Snow Queen.

The Third Story,

The Flower Garden of the Woman Who Could Conjure

BUT how fared little Gerda during Kay's absence? What had become of him, no one knew, nor could any one give the slightest information, excepting the boys, who said that he had tied his sledge to another very large one, which had driven through the street, and out at the town gate. Nobody knew where it went; many tears were shed for him, and little Gerda wept bitterly for a long time. She said she knew he must be dead; that he was drowned in the river which flowed close by the school. Oh, indeed those long winter days were very dreary. But at last spring came, with warm sunshine. "Kay is dead and gone," said little Gerda.

"I don't believe it," said the sunshine.

"He is dead and gone," she said to the sparrows.

"We don't believe it," they replied; and at last little Gerda began to doubt it herself. "I will put on my new red shoes," she said one morning, "those that Kay has never seen, and then I will go down to the river, and ask for him."

It was quite early when she kissed her old grandmother, who was still asleep; then she put on her red shoes, and went quite alone out of the town gates toward the river. "Is it true that you have taken my little playmate away from me?" said she to the river. "I will give you my red shoes if you will give him back to me." And it seemed as if the waves nodded to her in a strange manner.

Then she took off her red shoes, which she liked better than anything else, and threw them both into the river, but they fell near the bank, and the little waves carried them back to the land, just as if the river would not take from her what she loved best, because they could not give her back little Kay.

But she thought the shoes had not been thrown out far enough. Then she crept into a boat that lay among the reeds, and threw the shoes again from the farther end of the boat into the water, but it was not fastened. And her movement sent it gliding away from the land. When she saw this she hastened to reach the end of the boat, but before she could so it was more than a yard from the bank, and drifting away faster than ever.

Then little Gerda was very much frightened, and began to cry, but no one heard her except the sparrows, and they could not carry her to land, but they flew along by the shore, and sang, as if to comfort her, "Here we are! Here we are!" The boat floated with the stream; little Gerda sat quite still with only her stockings on her feet; the red shoes floated after her, but she could not reach them because the boat kept so much in advance.

The banks on each side of the river were very pretty. There were beautiful flowers, old trees, sloping fields, in which cows and sheep were grazing, but not a man to be seen.

Perhaps the river will carry me to little Kay, thought Gerda, and then she became more cheerful, and raised her head, and looked at the beautiful green banks; and so the boat sailed on for hours. At length she came to a large cherry orchard, in which stood a small red house with strange red and blue windows. It had also a thatched roof, and outside were two wooden soldiers, that presented arms to her as she sailed past. Gerda called out to them, for she thought they were alive, but of course they did not answer; and as the boat drifted nearer to the shore, she saw what they really were. Then Gerda called still louder, and there came a very old woman out of the house, leaning on a crutch. She wore a large hat to shade her from the sun, and on it were painted all sorts of pretty flowers.

"You poor little child," said the old woman, "how did you manage to come all this distance into the wide world on such a rapid rolling stream?" And then the old woman walked in the water, seized the boat with her crutch, drew it to land, and lifted Gerda out. And Gerda was glad to feel herself on dry ground, although she was rather afraid of the strange old woman.

"Come and tell me who you are," said she, "and how came you here."

Then Gerda told her everything, while the old woman shook her head, and said, "Hem-hem;" and when she had finished, Gerda asked if she had not seen little Kay, and the old woman told her he had not passed by that way, but he very likely would come. So she told Gerda not to be sorrowful, but to taste the cherries and look at the flowers; they were better than any picture-book, for each of them could tell a story.

Then she took Gerda by the hand and led her into the little house, and the old woman closed the door. The windows were very high, and as the panes were red, blue, and yellow, the daylight shone through them in all sorts of singular colors. On the table stood beautiful cherries, and Gerda had permission to eat as many as she would.

While she was eating them the old woman combed out her long flaxen ringlets with a golden comb, and the glossy curls hung down on each side of the little round pleasant face, which looked fresh and blooming as a rose. "I have long been wishing for a dear little maiden like you," said the old woman, "and now you must stay with me, and see how happily we shall live together."

And while she went on combing little Gerda's hair, she thought less and less about her adopted brother Kay, for the old woman could conjure, although she was not a wicked witch; she conjured only a little for her own amusement, and now, because she wanted to keep Gerda. Therefore she went into the garden, and stretched out her crutch towards all the rose-trees, beautiful though they were; and they immediately sunk into the dark earth, so that no one could tell where they had once stood. The old woman was afraid that if little Gerda saw roses she would think of those at home, and then remember little Kay, and run away.

Then she took Gerda into the flower-garden. How fragrant and beautiful it was! Every flower that could be thought of for every season of the year was here in full bloom; no picture-book could have more beautiful colors. Gerda jumped for joy, and played till the sun went down behind the tall cherry-trees; then she slept in an elegant bed with red silk pillows, embroidered with colored violets; and then she dreamed as pleasantly as a queen on her wedding day.

The next day, and for many days after, Gerda played with the flowers in the warm sunshine. She knew every flower, and yet, although there were so many of them, it seemed as if one were missing, but which it was she could not tell. One day, however, as she sat looking at the old woman's hat with the painted flowers on it, she saw that the prettiest of them all was a rose. The old woman had forgotten to take it from her hat when she made all the roses sink into the earth. But it is difficult to keep the thoughts together in everything; one little mistake upsets all our arrangements.

"What, are there no roses here?" cried Gerda; and she ran out into the garden, and examined all the beds, and searched and searched. There was not one to be found. Then she sat down and wept, and her tears fell just on the place where one of the rose-trees had sunk down. The warm tears moistened the earth, and the rose-tree sprouted up at once, as blooming as when it had sunk; and Gerda embraced it and kissed the roses, and thought of the beautiful roses at home, and, with them, of little Kay.

"Oh, how I have been detained!" said the little maiden, "I wanted to seek for little Kay. Do you know where he is?" she asked the roses; "do you think he is dead?"

And the Roses answered, *"No, he is not dead. We have been in the ground where all the dead lie; but Kay is not there."*

"Thank you," said little Gerda, and then she went to the other flowers, and looked into their little cups, and asked, "Do you know where little Kay is?" But each flower, as it stood in the sunshine, dreamed only of its own little fairy tale of history. Not one knew anything of Kay. Gerda heard many stories from the flowers, as she asked them one after another about him.

And what said the Tiger-lily? *"Hark, do you hear the drum?— 'tum, tum,'—there are only two notes, always, 'tum, tum.' Listen to the women's song of mourning! Hear the cry of the priest! In her long red robe stands the Hindoo widow by the funeral pile. The flames rise around her as she places herself on the dead body of her husband; but the Hindoo woman is thinking of the living one in that circle; of him, her son, who lighted those flames. Those shining eyes trouble her heart more painfully than the flames which will soon consume her body to ashes. Can the fire of the heart be extinguished in the flames of the funeral pile?"*

"I don't understand that at all," said little Gerda.

"That is my story," said the tiger-lily.

What says the Convolvulus? *"Near yonder narrow road stands an old knight's castle; thick ivy creeps over the old ruined walls, leaf over leaf, even to the balcony, in which stands a beautiful maiden. She bends over the balustrades, and looks up the road. No rose on its stem is fresher than she; no apple-blossom, wafted by the wind, floats more lightly than she moves. Her rich silk rustles as she bends over and exclaims, 'Will he not come?'*

"Is it Kay you mean?" asked Gerda.

"I am only speaking of a story of my dream," replied the flower.

What said the little Snow-drop? *"Between two trees a rope is hanging; there is a piece of board upon it; it is a swing. Two pretty little girls, in dresses white as snow, and with long green ribbons fluttering from their hats, are sitting upon it swinging. Their brother who is taller than they are, stands in the swing; he has one arm round the rope, to steady himself; in one hand he holds a little bowl, and in the other a clay pipe; he is blowing bubbles. As the swing goes on, the bubbles fly upward, reflecting the most beautiful varying colors. The last still hangs from the bowl of the pipe, and sways in the wind. On goes the swing; and then a little black dog comes running up. He is almost as light as the bubble, and he raises himself on his hind legs, and wants to be taken into the swing; but it does not stop, and the dog falls; then he barks and gets angry. The children stoop towards him, and the bubble bursts. A swinging plank, a light sparkling foam picture,—that is my story."*

"It may be all very pretty what you are telling me," said little Gerda, "but you speak so mournfully, and you do not mention little Kay at all."

What do the Hyacinths say? *"There were three beautiful sisters, fair and delicate. The dress of one was red, of the second blue, and of the third pure white. Hand in hand they danced in the bright moonlight, by the calm* lake; but they were human beings, not fairy elves. The sweet fragrance attracted them, and they disappeared in the wood; here the fragrance became stronger. Three coffins, in which lay the three beautiful maidens, glided from the thickest part of the forest across the lake. The fire-flies flew lightly over them, like little floating torches. Do the dancing maidens sleep, or are they dead? The scent of the flower says that they are corpses. The evening bell tolls their knell."

"You make me quite sorrowful," said little Gerda; "your perfume is so strong, you make me think of the dead maidens. Ah! is little Kay really dead then? The roses have been in the earth, and they say no."

"Cling, clang," tolled the Hyacinth bells. "We are not tolling for little Kay; we do not know him. We sing our song, the only one we know."

Then Gerda went to the buttercups that were glittering amongst the bright green leaves.

"You are little bright suns," said Gerda; "tell me if you know where I can find my play-fellow."

And the Buttercups sparkled gayly, and looked again at Gerda. What song could the Buttercups sing? It was not about Kay.

"The bright warm sun shone on a little court, on the first warm day of spring. His bright beams rested on the white walls of the neighboring house; and close by bloomed the first yellow flower of the season, glittering like gold in the sun's warm ray. An old woman sat in her arm chair at the house door, and her granddaughter, a poor and pretty servant-maid came to see her for a short visit. When she kissed her grandmother there was gold everywhere: the gold of the heart in that holy kiss; it was a golden morn-

ing; there was gold in the beaming sunlight, gold in the leaves of the lowly flower, and on the lips of the maiden. There, that is my story," said the Buttercup.

"My poor old grandmother!" sighed Gerda; "she is longing to see me, and grieving for me as she did for little Kay; but I shall soon go home now, and take little Kay with me. It is no use asking the flowers; they know only their own songs, and can give me no information."

And then she tucked up her little dress, that she might run faster, but the narcissus caught her by the leg as she was jumping over it; so she stopped and looked at the tall yellow flower, and said, "Perhaps you may know something."

Then she stooped down quite close to the flower, and listened; and what did he say?

"I can see myself, I can see myself," said the narcissus. *"Oh, how sweet is my perfume! Up in a little room with a bow window, stands a little dancing girl, half undressed; she stands sometimes on one leg, and sometimes on both, and looks as if she would tread the whole world under her feet. She is nothing but a delusion. She is pouring water out of a tea-pot on a piece of stuff which she holds in her hand; it is her bodice. 'Cleanliness is a good thing,' she says. Her white dress hangs on a peg; it has also been washed in the tea-pot, and dried on the roof. She puts it on, and ties a saffron-colored handkerchief round her neck, which makes the dress look whiter. See how she stretches out her legs, as if she were showing off on a stem. I can see myself, I can see myself."*

"What do I care for all that," said Gerda, "you need not tell me such stuff." And then she ran to the other end of the garden. The door was fastened, but she pressed against the rusty latch, and it gave way. The door sprang open, and little Gerda ran out with bare feet into the wide world. She looked back three times, but no one seemed to be following her. At last she could run no longer, so she sat down to rest on a great stone, and when she looked round she saw that the summer was over, and autumn very far advanced. She had known nothing of this in the beautiful garden, where the sun shone and the flowers grew all the year round.

"Oh, how I have wasted my time?" said little Gerda; "it is autumn. I must not rest any longer," and she rose up to go on. But her little feet were wounded and sore, and everything around her looked so cold and bleak. The long willow-leaves were quite yellow.

The dew-drops fell like water, leaf after leaf dropped from the trees, the sloe-thorn alone still bore fruit, but the sloes were sour, and set the teeth on edge. Oh, how dark and weary the whole world appeared!

Fourth Story,

The Prince and Princess

GERDA was obliged to rest again, and just opposite the place where she sat, she saw a great crow come hopping across the snow toward her. He stood looking at her for some time, and then he wagged his head and said, "Caw, caw; good-day, good-day." He pronounced the words as plainly as he could, because he meant to be kind to the little girl; and then he asked her where she was going all alone in the wide world.

The word alone Gerda understood very well, and knew how much it expressed. So then she told the crow the whole story of her life and adventures, and asked him if he had seen little Kay.

The crow nodded his head very gravely, and said, "Perhaps I have—it may be."

"No! Do you think you have?" cried little Gerda, and she kissed the crow, and hugged him almost to death with joy.

"Gently, gently," said the crow. "I believe I know. I think it may be little Kay; but he has certainly forgotten you by this time for the princess."

"Does he live with a princess?" asked Gerda.

"Yes, listen," replied the crow, "but it is so difficult to speak your language. If you understand the crows' language[1] then I can explain it better. Do you?"

---

[1] Children have a kind of a language, or gibberish, which is sometimes called "crow's language;" it is formed by adding letters or syllables to every word.

"No, I have never learnt it," said Gerda, "but my grandmother understands it, and used to speak it to me. I wish I had learnt it."

"It does not matter," answered the crow; "I will explain as well as I can, although it will be very badly done;" and he told her what he had heard. "In this kingdom where we now are," said he, "there lives a princess, who is so wonderfully clever that she has read all the newspapers in the world, and forgotten them too, although she is so clever. A short time ago, as she was sitting on her throne, which people say is not such an agreeable seat as is often supposed, she began to sing a song which commences in these words:

'Why should I not be married?'
'Why not indeed?' said she, and so she determined to marry if she could find a husband who knew what to

say when he was spoken to, and not one who could only look grand, for that was so tiresome. Then she assembled all her court ladies together at the beat of the drum, and when they heard of her intentions they were very much pleased. 'We are so glad to hear it,' said they, 'we were talking about it ourselves the other day.' You may believe that every word I tell you is true," said the crow, "for I have a tame sweetheart who goes freely about the palace, and she told me all this."

Of course his sweetheart was a crow, for "birds of a feather flock together," and one crow always chooses another crow.

"Newspapers were published immediately, with a border of hearts, and the initials of the princess among them. They gave notice that every young man who was handsome was free to visit the castle and speak with the princess; and those who could reply loud enough to be heard when spoken to, were to make themselves quite at home at the palace; but the one who spoke best would be chosen as a husband for the princess. Yes, yes, you may believe me, it is all as true as I sit here," said the crow.

"The people came in crowds. There was a great deal of crushing and running about, but no one succeeded either on the first or second day. They could all speak very well while they were outside in the streets, but when they entered the palace gates, and saw the guards in silver uniforms, and the footmen in their golden livery on the staircase, and the great halls lighted up, they became quite confused. And when they stood before the throne on which the princess sat, they could do nothing but repeat the last words she had said; and she had no particular wish to hear her own words over again. It was just as if they had all taken something to make them sleepy while they were in the palace, for they did not recover themselves nor speak till they got back again into the street. There was quite a long line of them reaching from the town-gate to the palace. I went myself to see them," said the crow.

"They were hungry and thirsty, for at the palace they did not get even a glass of water. Some of the wisest had taken a few slices of bread and butter with them, but they did not share it with their neighbors; they thought if they went in to the princess looking hungry, there would be a better chance for themselves."

"But Kay! tell me about little Kay!" said Gerda, "was he amongst the crowd?"

"Stop a bit, we are just coming to him. It was on the third day, there came marching cheerfully along to the palace a little personage, without horses or carriage, his eyes sparkling like yours; he had beautiful long hair, but his clothes were very poor."

"That was Kay!" said Gerda joyfully. "Oh, then I have found him;" and she clapped her hands.

"He had a little knapsack on his back," added the crow.

"No, it must have been his sledge," said Gerda; "for he went away with it."

"It may have been so," said the crow; "I did not look at it very closely. But I know from my tame sweetheart that he passed through the palace gates, saw the guards in their silver uniform, and the servants in their liveries of gold on the stairs, but he was not in the least embarrassed. 'It must be very tiresome to stand on the stairs,' he said. 'I prefer to go in.' The rooms were blazing with light. Councillors and ambassadors walked about with bare feet, carrying golden vessels; it was enough to make any one feel serious. His boots creaked loudly as he walked, and yet he was not at all uneasy."

"It must be Kay," said Gerda, "I know he had new boots on, I have heard them creak in grandmother's room."

"They really did creak," said the crow, "yet he went boldly up to the princess herself, who was sitting on a pearl as large as a spinning wheel, and all the ladies of the court were present with their maids, and all the cavaliers with their servants; and each of the maids had another maid to wait upon her, and the cavaliers' servants had their own servants, as well as a page each. They all stood in circles round the princess, and the nearer they stood to the door, the prouder they looked. The servants' pages, who always wore slippers, could hardly be looked at, they held themselves up so proudly by the door."

"It must be quite awful," said little Gerda, "but did Kay win the princess?"

"If I had not been a crow," said he, "I would have married her myself, although I am engaged. He spoke just as well as I do, when I speak the crows' language, so I heard from my tame sweetheart. He was quite free and agreeable and said he had not come to woo the princess, but to hear her wisdom; and he was as pleased with her as she was with him."

"Oh, certainly that was Kay," said Gerda, "he was so clever; he could work mental arithmetic and fractions. Oh, will you take me to the palace?"

"It is very easy to ask that," replied the crow, "but how are we to manage it? However, I will speak about it to my tame sweetheart, and ask her advice; for I must tell you it will be very difficult to gain permission for a little girl like you to enter the palace."

"Oh, yes; but I shall gain permission easily," said Gerda, "for when Kay hears that I am here, he will come out and fetch me in immediately."

"Wait for me here by the palings," said the crow, wagging his head as he flew away.

It was late in the evening before the crow returned.

"Caw, caw," he said, "she sends you greeting, and here is a little roll which she took from the kitchen for you; there is plenty of bread there, and she thinks you must be hungry. It is not possible for you to enter the palace by the front entrance. The guards in silver uniform and the servants in gold livery would not allow it. But do not cry, we will manage to get you in; my sweetheart knows a little back-staircase that leads to the sleeping apartments, and she knows where to find the key."

Then they went into the garden through the great avenue, where the leaves were falling one after another, and they could see the light in the palace being put out in the same manner. And the crow led little Gerda to the back door, which stood ajar. Oh! how little Gerda's heart beat with anxiety and longing; it was just as if she were going to do something wrong, and yet she only wanted to know where little Kay was. "It must be he," she thought, "with those clear eyes, and that long hair." She could fancy she saw him smiling at her, as he used to at home, when they sat among the roses. He would certainly be glad to see her, and to hear what a long distance she had come for his sake, and to know how sorry they had been at home because he did not come back. Oh what joy and yet fear she felt! They were now on the stairs, and in a small closet at the top a lamp was burning. In the middle of the floor stood the tame crow, turning her head from side to side, and gazing at Gerda, who curtseyed as her grandmother had taught her to do.

"My betrothed has spoken so very highly of you, my little lady," said the tame crow, "your life-history, *Vita*, as it may be called, is very touching. If you will take the lamp I will walk before you. We will go straight along this way, then we shall meet no one."

"It seems to me as if somebody were behind us," said Gerda, as something rushed by her like a shadow on the wall, and then horses with flying manes and thin legs, hunters, ladies and gentlemen on horseback, glided by her, like shadows on the wall.

"They are only dreams," said the crow, "they are coming to fetch the thoughts of the great people out hunting."

"All the better, for we shall be able to look at them in their beds more safely. I hope that when you rise to honor and favor, you will show a grateful heart."

"You may be quite sure of that," said the crow from the forest.

They now came into the first hall, the walls of which were hung with rose-colored satin, embroidered with artificial flowers. Here the dreams again flitted by them but so quickly that Gerda could not distinguish the royal persons. Each hall appeared more splendid than the last, it was enought to bewilder any one. At length they reached a bedroom. The ceiling was like a great palm-tree, with glass leaves of the most costly crystal, and over the centre of the floor two beds, each resembling a lily, hung from a stem of gold. One, in which the princess lay, was white, the other was red; and in this Gerda had to seek for little Kay. She pushed one of the red leaves aside, and saw a little brown neck. Oh, that must be Kay! She called his name out quite loud, and held the lamp over him. The dreams rushed back into the room on horseback.

He woke, and turned his head round, it was not little Kay! The prince was only like him in the neck, still he was young and pretty. Then the princess peeped out of her white-lily bed, and asked what was the matter. Then little Gerda wept and told her story, and all that the crows had done to help her.

"You poor child," said the prince and princess; then they praised the crows, and said they were not angry for what they had done, but that it must not happen again, and this time they should be rewarded.

"Would you like to have your freedom?" asked the princess, "or would you prefer to be raised to the position of court crows, with all that is left in the kitchen for yourselves?"

Then both the crows bowed, and begged to have a fixed appointment, for they thought of their old age, and said it would be so comfortable to feel that they had provision for their old days, as they called it. And then the prince got out of his bed, and gave it up to Gerda,—he could do no more; and she lay down. She folded her little hands, and thought, "How good everyone is to me, men and animals too;" then she closed her eyes and fell into a sweet sleep. All the dreams came flying back again to her, and they looked like angels, and one of them drew a little sledge, on which sat Kay, and nodded to her. But all this was only a dream, and vanished as soon as she awoke.

The following day she was dressed from head to foot in silk and velvet, and they invited her to stay at the palace for a few days, and enjoy herself, but she only begged for a pair of boots, and a little carriage, and a horse to draw it, so that she might go into the wide world to seek for Kay. And she obtained, not only boots, but also a muff, and she was neatly dressed; and when she was ready to go, there, at the door, she

found a coach made of pure gold, with the coat-of-arms of the prince and princess shining upon it like a star, and the coachman, footman, and outriders all wearing golden crowns on their heads. The prince and princess themselves helped her into the coach, and wished her success.

The forest crow, who was now married, accompanied her for the first three miles; he sat by Gerda's side, as he could not bear riding backwards. The tame crow stood in the door-way flapping her wings. She could not go with them, because she had been suffering from headache ever since the new appointment, no doubt from eating too much. The coach was well stored with sweet cakes, and under the seat were fruit and gingerbread nuts.

"Farewell, farewell," cried the prince and princess, and little Gerda wept, and the crow wept; and then, after a few miles, the crow also said "Farewell," and this was the saddest parting. However, he flew to a tree, and stood flapping his black wings as long as he could see the coach, which glittered in the bright sunshine.

Fifth Story,

Little Robber-Girl

THE coach drove on through a thick forest, where it lighted up the way like a torch, and dazzled the eyes of some robbers, who could not bear to let it pass them unmolested.

"It is gold! it is gold!" cried they, rushing forward, and seizing the horses. Then they struck the little jockeys, the coachman, and the footman dead, and pulled little Gerda out of the carriage.

"She is fat and pretty, and she has been fed with the kernels of nuts," said the old robber-woman, who had a long beard and eyebrows that hung over her eyes. "She is as good as a little lamb; how nice she will taste!" and as she said this, she drew forth a shining knife, that glittered horribly. "Oh!" screamed the old woman the same moment; for her own daughter, who held her back, had bitten her in the ear. She was a wild and naughty girl, and the mother called her an ugly thing, and had not time to kill Gerda.

"She shall play with me," said the little robber-girl; "she shall give me her muff and her pretty dress, and sleep with me in my bed." And then she bit her mother again, and made her spring in the air, and jump about; and all the robbers laughed, and said, "See how she is dancing with her young cub."

"I will have a ride in the coach," said the little robber-girl; and she would have her own way; for she was so self-willed and obstinate.

She and Gerda seated themselves in the coach, and drove away, over stumps and stones, into the depths of the forest. The little robber-girl was about the same size as Gerda, but stronger; she had broader shoulders and a darker skin; her eyes were quite black, and she had a mournful look. She clasped little Gerda round the waist, and said,—

"They shall not kill you as long as you don't make us vexed with you. I suppose you are a princess."

"No," said Gerda; and then she told her all her history, and how fond she was of little Kay.

The robber-girl looked earnestly at her, nodded her head slightly, and said, "They sha'nt kill you, even if

I do get angry with you; for I will do it myself." And then she wiped Gerda's eyes, and stuck her own hands in the beautiful muff which was so soft and warm.

The coach stopped in the courtyard of a robber's castle, the walls of which were cracked from top to bottom. Ravens and crows flew in and out of the holes and crevices, while great bulldogs, either of which looked as if it could swallow a man, were jumping about; but they were not allowed to bark. In the large and smoky hall a bright fire was burning on the stone floor. There was no chimney; so the smoke went up to the ceiling, and found a way out for itself. Soup was boiling in a large cauldron, and hares and rabbits were roasting on the spit.

"You shall sleep with me and all my little animals to-night," said the robber-girl, after they had had something to eat and drink. So she took Gerda to a corner of the hall, where some straw and carpets were laid down. Above them, on laths and perches, were more than a hundred pigeons, who all seemed to be asleep, although they moved slightly when the two little girls came near them.

"These all belong to me," said the robber-girl; and she seized the nearest to her, held it by the feet, and shook it till it flapped its wings. "Kiss it," cried she, flapping it in Gerda's face. "There sit the wood-pigeons," continued she, pointing to a number of laths and a cage which had been fixed into the walls, near one of the openings. "Both rascals would fly away directly, if they were not closely locked up. And here is my old sweetheart 'Ba;'" and she dragged out a reindeer by the horn; he wore a bright copper ring round his neck, and was tied up. "We are obliged to hold him tight too, or else he would run away from us also. I tickle his neck every evening with my sharp knife, which frightens him very much." And then the robber-girl drew a long knife from a chink in the wall, and let it slide gently over the reindeer's neck. The poor animal began to kick, and the little robber-girl laughed, and pulled down Gerda into bed with her.

"Will you have that knife with you while you are asleep?" asked Gerda, looking at it in great fright.

"I always sleep with the knife by me," said the robber-girl. "No one knows what may happen. But now tell me again all about little Kay, and why you went out into the world."

Then Gerda repeated her story over again, while the wood-pigeons in the cage over her cooed, and the other pigeons slept. The little robber-girl put one arm across Gerda's neck, and held the knife in the other, and was soon fast asleep and snoring. But Gerda could not close her eyes at all; she knew not whether she was to live or die. The robbers sat round the fire, singing and drinking, and the old woman stumbled about. It was a terrible sight for a little girl to witness.

Then the wood-pigeons said, "Coo, coo; we have seen little Kay. A white fowl carried his sledge, and he sat in the carriage of the Snow Queen, which drove through the wood while we were lying in our nest. She blew upon us, and all the young ones died excepting us two. Coo, coo."

"What are you saying up there?" cried Gerda. "Where was the Snow Queen going? Do you know anything about it?"

"She was most likely travelling to Lapland, where there is always snow and ice. Ask the reindeer that is fastened up there with a rope."

"Yes, there is always snow and ice," said the reindeer; "and it is a glorious place; you can leap and run about freely on the sparkling ice plains. The Snow Queen has her summer tent there, but her strong castle is at the North Pole, on an island called Spitzbergen."

"Oh, Kay, little Kay!" sighed Gerda.

"Lie still," said the robber-girl, "or I shall run my knife into your body."

In the morning Gerda told her all that the wood-pigeons had said; and the little robber-girl looked quite serious, and nodded her head, and said, "That is all talk, that is all talk. Do you know where Lapland is?" she asked the reindeer.

"Who should know better than I do?" said the animal, while his eyes sparkled. "I was born and brought up there, and used to run about the snow-covered plains."

"Now listen," said the robber-girl; "all our men are gone away,— only mother is here, and here she will stay; but at noon she always drinks out of a great bottle, and afterwards sleeps for a little while; and then, I'll do something for you." Then she jumped out of bed, clasped her mother round the neck, and pulled her by the beard, crying, "My own little nanny goat, good morning." Then her mother filliped her nose till it was quite red; yet she did it all for love.

When the mother had drunk out of the bottle, and was gone to sleep, the little robber-maiden went to the reindeer, and said, "I should like very much to tickle your neck a few times more with my knife, for it makes you look so funny; but never mind,—I will untie your cord, and set you free, so that you may run away to Lapland; but you must make good use of your legs, and carry this little maiden to the castle of the Snow Queen, where her play-fellow is. You have heard what she told me, for she spoke loud enough, and you were listening."

Then the reindeer jumped for joy; and the little robber-girl lifted Gerda on his back, and had the fore-thought to tie her on, and even to give her her own little cushion to sit on.

"Here are your fur boots for you," said she; "for it will be very cold; but I must keep the muff; it is so pretty. However, you shall not be frozen for the want of it; here are my mother's large warm mittens; they will reach up to your elbows. Let me put them on. There, now your hands look just like my mother's."

But Gerda wept for joy.

"I don't like to see you fret," said the little robber-girl; "you ought to look quite happy now; and here are two loaves and a ham, so that you need not starve." These were fastened on the reindeer, and then the little robber-maiden opened the door, coaxed in all the great dogs, and then cut the string with which the reindeer was fastened, with her sharp knife, and said, "Now run, but mind you take good care of the little girl." And then Gerda stretched out her hand, with the great mitten on it, towards the little robber-girl, and said, "Farewell," and away flew the reindeer, over stumps and stones, through the great forest, over marshes and plains, as quickly as he could. The

wolves howled, and the ravens screamed; while up in the sky quivered red lights like flames of fire. "There are my old northern lights," said the reindeer; "see how they flash." And he ran on day and night still faster and faster, but the loaves and the ham were all eaten by the time they reached Lapland.

Sixth Story,

The Lapland Woman and
the Finland Woman

HEY stopped at a little hut; it was very mean looking; the roof sloped nearly down to the ground, and the door was so low that the family had to creep in on their hands and knees, when they went in and out. There was no one at home but an old Lapland woman, who was cooking fish by the light of a train-oil lamp. The reindeer told her all about Gerda's story, after having first told his own, which seemed to him the most important, but Gerda was so pinched with the cold that she could not speak.

"Oh, you poor things," said the Lapland woman, "you have a long way to go yet. You must travel more than a hundred miles farther, to Finland. The Snow Queen lives there now, and she burns Bengal lights every evening. I will write a few words on a dried stock-fish, for I have no paper, and you can take it from me to the Finland woman who lives there; she can give you better information than I can."

So when Gerda was warmed, and had taken something to eat and drink, the woman wrote a few words on the dried fish, and told Gerda to take great care of it. Then she tied her again on the reindeer, and he set off at full speed. Flash, flash, went the beautiful blue northern lights in the air the whole night long. And at length they reached Finland, and knocked at the chimney of the Finland woman's hut, for it had no door above the ground. They crept in, but it was so terribly hot inside that that woman wore scarcely any clothes; she was small and very dirty looking.

She loosened little Gerda's dress, and took off the fur boots and the mittens, or Gerda would have been unable to bear the heat; and then she placed a piece of ice on the reindeer's head, and read what was written on the dried fish. After she had read it three times, she knew it by heart, so she popped the fish into the soup saucepan, as she knew it was good to eat, and she never wasted anything.

The reindeer told his own story first, and then little Gerda's, and the Finlander twinkled with her clever eyes, but she said nothing. "You are so clever," said the reindeer; "I know you can tie all the winds of the world with a piece of twine. If a sailor unties one knot, he has a fair wind; when he unties the second, it blows hard; but if the third and fourth are loosened, then comes a storm, which will root up whole forests. Cannot you give this little maiden something which will make her as strong as twelve men, to overcome the Snow Queen?"

"The Power of twelve men!" said the Finland woman; "that would be of very little use." But she went to a shelf and took down and unrolled a large skin, on which were inscribed wonderful characters, and she read till the perspiration ran down from her forehead. But the reindeer begged so hard for little Gerda, and Gerda looked at the Finland woman with such beseeching tearful eyes, that her own eyes began to twinkle again; so she drew the reindeer into a corner, and whispered to him while she laid a fresh piece of ice on his head, "Little Kay is really with the Snow Queen, but he finds everything there so much to his taste and his liking, that he believes it is the finest place in the world; but this is because he has a piece of broken glass in his heart, and a little piece of glass in his eye. These must be taken out, or he will never be a human being again, and the Snow Queen will retain her power over him."

"But can you not give little Gerda something to help her to conquer this power?"

"I can give her no greater power than she has already," said the woman; "don't you see how strong that is? How men and animals are obliged to serve her, and how well she has got through the world, barefooted as she is. She cannot receive any power from me greater than she now has, which consists in her own purity and innocence of heart. If she cannot herself obtain access to the Snow Queen, and remove the glass fragments from little Kay, we can do nothing to help her. Two miles from here the Snow Queen's garden begins; you can carry the little girl so far, and set her down by the large bush which stands in the snow, covered with red berries. Do not stay gossiping, but come back here as quickly as you can." Then the Finland woman lifted little Gerda upon the reindeer, and he ran away with her as quickly as he could.

"Oh, I have forgotten my boots and my mittens," cried little Gerda, as soon as she felt the cutting cold, but the reindeer dared not stop, so he ran on till he reached the bush with the red berries; here he set

Gerda down, and he kissed her, and the great bright tears trickled over the animal's cheeks; then he left her and ran back as fast as he could.

There stood poor Gerda, without shoes, without gloves, in the midst of cold, dreary, ice-bound Finland. She ran forwards as quickly as she could, when a whole regiment of snow-flakes came round her; they did not, however, fall from the sky, which was quite clear and glittering with the northern lights. The snow-flakes ran along the ground, and the nearer they came to her, the larger they appeared. Gerda remembered how large and beautiful they looked through the burning-glass. But these were really larger, and much more terrible, for they were alive, and were the guards of the Snow Queen, and had the strangest shapes. Some were like great porcupines, others like twisted serpents with their heads stretching out, and some few were like little fat bears with their hair bristled; but all were dazzlingly white, and all were living snow-flakes.

Then little Gerda repeated the Lord's Prayer, and the cold was so great that she could see her own breath come out of her mouth like steam as she uttered the words. The steam appeared to increase, as she continued her prayer, till it took the shape of little angels who grew larger the moment they touched the earth. They all wore helmets on their heads, and carried spears and shields. Their number continued to increase more and more; and by the time Gerda had finished her prayers, a whole legion stood round her. They thrust their spears into the terrible snow-flakes, so that they shivered into a hundred pieces, and little Gerda could go forward with courage and safety. The angels stroked her hands and feet, so that she felt the cold less, and she hastened on to the Snow Queen's castle.

But now we must see what Kay is doing. In truth he thought not of little Gerda, and never supposed she could be standing in the front of the palace.

Seventh Story,

Of the Palace of the Snow Queen and What Happened There at Last

The walls of the palace were formed of drifted snow, and the windows and doors of the cutting winds. There were more than a hundred rooms in it, all as if they had been formed with snow blown together. The largest of them extended for several miles; they were all lighted up by the vivid light of the aurora, and they were so large and empty, so icy cold and glittering! There were no amusements here, not even a little bear's ball, when the storm might have been the music, and the bears could have danced on their hind legs, and shown their good manners. There were no pleasant games of snap-dragon, or touch, or even a gossip over the tea-table, for the young-lady foxes. Empty, vast, and cold were the halls of the Snow Queen. The flickering flame of the northern lights could be plainly seen, whether they rose high or low in the heavens, from every part of the castle. In the midst of its empty, endless hall of snow was a frozen lake, broken on its surface into a thousand forms; each piece resembled another, from being in itself perfect as a work of art, and in the centre of this lake sat the Snow Queen, when she was at home. She called the lake "The Mirror of Reason," and said that it was the best, and indeed the only one in the world.

Little Kay was quite blue with cold, indeed almost black, but he did not feel it; for the Snow Queen had kissed away the icy shiverings, and his heart was already a lump of ice. He dragged some sharp, flat pieces of ice to and fro, and placed them together in all kinds of positions, as if he wished to make something out of them; just as we try to form various figures with little tablets of wood which we call "a

Chinese puzzle." Kay's fingers were very artistic; it was the icy game of reason at which he played, and in his eyes the figures were very remarkable, and of the highest importance; this opinion was owing to the piece of glass still sticking in his eye. He composed many complete figures, forming different words, but there was one word he never could manage to form, although he wished it very much. It was the word "Eternity." The Snow Queen had said to him, "When you can find out this, you shall be your own master, and I will give you the whole world and a new pair of skates." But he could not accomplish it.

"Now I must hasten away to warmer countries," said the Snow Queen. "I will go and look into the black craters of the tops of the burning mountains, Etna and Vesuvius, as they are called,—I shall make them look white, which will be good for them, and for the lemons and the grapes." And away flew the Snow Queen, leaving little Kay quite alone in the great hall which was so many miles in length; so he sat and looked at his pieces of ice, and was thinking so deeply, and sat so still, that any one might have supposed he was frozen.

Just at this moment it happened that little Gerda came through the great door of the castle. Cutting winds were raging around her, but she offered up a prayer and the winds sank down as if they were going to sleep; and she went on till she came to the large empty hall, and caught sight of Kay; she knew him directly; she flew to him and threw her arms round his neck, and held him fast, while she exclaimed, "Kay, dear little Kay, I have found you at last."

But he sat quite still, stiff and cold.

Then little Gerda wept hot tears, which fell on his breast, and penetrated into his heart, and thawed the lump of ice, and washed away the little piece of glass which had stuck there. Then he looked at her, and she sang—

> "Roses bloom and cease to be,
> But we shall the Christ-child see."

Then Kay burst into tears, and he wept so that the splinter of glass swam out of his eye. Then he recognized Gerda, and said, joyfully, "Gerda, dear little Gerda, where have you been all this time, and where have I been?" And he looked all around him, and said, "How cold it is, and how large and empty it all looks," and he clung to Gerda, and she laughed and wept for joy. It was so pleasing to see them that the pieces of ice even danced about; and when they were tired and went to lie down, they formed themselves into the letters of the word which the Snow Queen had said he must find out before he could be his own master, and have the whole world and a pair of new skates.

Then Gerda kissed his cheeks, and they became blooming; and she kissed his eyes, and they shone like her own; she kissed his hands and his feet, and then he became quite healthy and cheerful. The Snow Queen might come home now when she pleased, for there stood his certainty of freedom, in the word she wanted, written in shining letters of ice.

Then they took each other by the hand, and went forth from the great palace of ice. They spoke of the grandmother, and of the roses on the roof, and as they went on the winds were at rest, and the sun burst forth. When they arrived at the bush with red berries, there stood the reindeer waiting for them, and he had brought another young reindeer with him, whose udders were full, and the children drank her warm milk and kissed her on the mouth.

Then they carried Kay and Gerda first to the Finland woman, where they warmed themselves thoroughly in the hot room, and she gave them directions about their journey home. Next they went to the Lapland woman, who had made some new clothes for them, and put their sleighs in order. Both the reindeer ran by their side, and followed them as far as the boundaries of the country, where the first green leaves were budding. And here they took leave of the two reindeer and the Lapland woman, and all said—Farewell.

Then the birds began to twitter, and the forest too was full of green young leaves; and out of it came a beautiful horse, which Gerda remembered, for it was one which had drawn the golden coach. A young girl was riding upon it, with a shining red cap on her head, and pistols in her belt. It was the little robber-maiden, who had got tired of staying at home; she was going first to the north, and if that did not suit her, she meant to try some other part of the world. She knew Gerda directly, and Gerda remembered her: it was a joyful meeting.

"You are a fine fellow to go gadding about in this way," said she to little Kay, "I should like to know whether you deserve that any one should go to the end of the world to find you."

But Gerda patted her cheeks, and asked after the prince and princess.

"They are gone to foreign countries," said the robber-girl.

"And the crow?" asked Gerda.

"Oh, the crow is dead," she replied; "his tame sweetheart is now a widow, and wears a bit of black worsted round her leg. She mourns very pitifully, but it is all stuff. But now tell me how you managed to get him back."

Then Gerda and Kay told her all about it.

"Snip, snap, snare! it's all right at last," said the robber-girl.

Then she took both their hands, and promised that if ever she should pass through the town, she would call and pay them a visit. And then she rode away into the wide world. But Gerda and Kay went hand-in-hand towards home; and as they advanced, spring appeared more lovely with its green verdure and its beautiful flowers. Very soon they recognized the large town where they lived, and the tall steeples of the churches, in which the sweet bells were ringing a merry peal as they entered it, and found their way to their grandmother's door. They went upstairs into the little room, where all looked just as it used to do.

The old clock was going "tick, tick," and the hands pointed to the time of day, but as they passed through the door into the room they perceived that they were both grown up, and become a man and woman. The roses out on the roof were in full bloom, and peeped in at the window; and there stood the little chairs, on which they had sat when children; and Kay and Gerda seated themselves each on their own chair, and held each other by the hand, while the cold empty grandeur of the Snow Queen's palace vanished from their memories like a painful dream.

The grandmother sat in God's bright sunshine, and she read aloud from the Bible, "Except ye become as little children, ye shall in no wise enter into the kingdom of God." And Kay and Gerda looked into each other's eyes, and all at once understood the words of the old song,

> "Roses bloom and cease to be,
> But we shall the Christ-child see."

And they both sat there, grown up, yet children at heart; and it was summer,—warm, beautiful summer.

Made in the USA
Lexington, KY
25 March 2014